The Princess in My Teacup

Sally Huss

ISBN: 0982262566
ISBN 13: 9780982262566

It happened awhile back while I was visiting my cousin.

We were having a cup of tea and eating cookies

By the dozen.

I was about to lift my cup to have another tasty swallow…

When my eye caught something that startled me

For what was to follow.

I looked into my teacup and to my astonishment and surprise

There was something there that shocked me,

I couldn't believe my eyes.

I thought, is that a princess in my teacup?

And why is she smiling up at me?

I'm just a little girl who is as simple as can be.

I do not know why she would visit me.

I do not know what is on her mind.

All I know is that she's very special

And I'll try to be most kind.

Of course, I could have told her all the things I do…

Like care for my dog and cat…

But when I opened my eyes again, the cup was gone

And that was that.

Then it happened once more

When I was lunching with a friend.

I looked into my soup bowl and found her back again.

She smiled at me and I smiled back.

Then I asked, "What can I do for you?"

She sighed and said, "Yes, there is something you can do.

It's really not much.

It is only that you should be useful…"

That gave me a hint, a hunch.

To be useful seemed a grown-up thing to do,

But I'd make an effort and see what I could do.

Each day I helped my mother with the kitchen chores –

And not just mine.

My mother thanked me and said how useful I was,

Which suited me just fine.

Then while we were cleaning up, I looked into the sink

And there was that face again. Who do you think?

Was that a princess in the sink smiling up at me again?

What now could she want from me?

I'll treat her like a friend.

I said, "Whatever can I do for you,

Dear princess whom I see?"

She answered, "You could be more grateful

For all the things you see."

"Grateful, yes. Sometimes I forget what a lucky girl I am."

"That's it," said the princess. "Now you've got the plan."

My mother pulled the plug and the water went down the sink

And away went the princess faster than I could blink.

The sink was not the last of her. No. No, not hardly.

It was when I was giving thanks for all the gifts

At my birthday party…

There floating happily in the bowl of punch

Was the princess who'd given me that last hunch?

Now what did she want? What could I do to please her?

She spoke, as a chunk of ice was added.

I hoped it wouldn't freeze her.

What she said was something I had never thought to do –

"Make friends with those who have none or very few."

Friends. Yes, I thought, I like to have many.

I thanked her for her suggestion

While someone, using the ladle, was making a punch selection

Which caused her to dissolve into a tasteful brew.

That was it; we seemed to be through.

Back at school on a very rainy day

I found a new friend when we went outside to play.

I had put on my galoshes and shared my umbrella

With a little boy who had been a very lonely fella.

We splashed in the water and danced in the rain

And we became good friends before we had to go inside again.

But before I left the schoolyard, I spotted a face in a puddle.

Goodness gracious, who would have expected a princess

To turn up in such a muddle?

But in the muddle she did

And thanked me for befriending that little kid.

Now what could she want me to do?

"Think kindly of others," she said, "they're just like you.

Not everything in their lives is perfect. See what you can do."

Of course I promised the princess I'd give it my all

And think kindly of others

Whether they were grumpy or mean, big or small.

Unfortunately someone stepped on the puddle on his way to class

And the princess disappeared with another big splash.

Back home again, I helped my mother prepare the evening meal,

Then gave thanks for the food before me and did it with great zeal.

I even told my family about my new friend

And all the while thought kindly of my brother and sister

'Till the dinner's end.

I got into the bath that night after filling up the tub,

Then opened my eyes, after giving my face a good scrub.

There she was, more glorious than before,

Then she thanked me for my efforts

And said that I could still do more.

I promised that I would.

I knew I would because it felt so good.

And that was our last goodbye,

But I had made a promise and I would try.

But who was that princess in the puddle of mud,

The kitchen sink, the bowl of soup, and the bathtub?

Why did she come and go, arrive and disappear?

I had to check my heart to make it clear.

And what it told me is something I will reveal to you

In case you come across a princess too.

The kindness and goodness that the princess asked me to share

Was something that I could easily spare.

I had plenty of it, plenty to give away

And that's what I promised to do each and every day.

That's how it all came about…

How I learned who the princess was, without a doubt.

Now I know that the princess in my cup of tea

Was none other than the princess in me!

The end,
but not the end of
being useful.

At the end of this book you will find a Certificate of Merit that may be issued to any girl who promises to honor the requirements stated in the Certificate. This fine Certificate will easily fit into a 5"x7" frame, and happily suit any girl who receives it!

Here is another adorable princess book by Sally Huss.

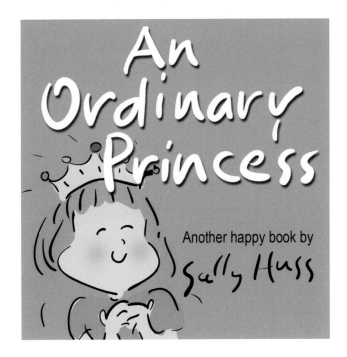

Synopsis: Laura Sue wanted to be a princess with all her heart. However, she was not from a royal family; she was from an ordinary family, which included an ordinary brother.

One day to her delight, her teacher announced to the students that they could be anything they wanted to be. This was music to Laura Sue's ears, until she announced her desire in front of the class. Laughter dampened her spirits, as did the reality that her family members offered. However, a beautiful, golden angel came to her rescue and told her how to become an ordinary princess. She gave her the formula and it is one every child could follow should he or she wish to become an ordinary prince or princess.

From AN ORDINARY PRINCESS --http://amzn.com/B00N1IR0IS.

If you liked THE PRINCESS IN MY TEACUP, please be kind enough to post a short review on Amazon by using this URL: http://amzn.com/B00NG4EDH8.

You may wish to join our Family of Friends to receive information about upcoming FREE e-book promotions and download a free poster – The Importance Happiness on Sally's website -- http://www.sallyhuss.com. Thank You.

More Sally Huss books may be viewed on the Author's Profile on Amazon. Here is that URL: http://amzn.to/VpR7B8.

About the Author/Illustrator

Sally Huss

"Bright and happy," "light and whimsical" have been the catch phrases attached to the writings and art of Sally Huss for over 30 years. Sweet images dance across all of Sally's creations, whether in the form of children's books, paintings, wallpaper, ceramics, baby bibs, purses, clothing, or her King Features Syndicated newspaper panel "Happy Musings."

Sally creates children's books to uplift the lives of children and hopes you will join in by helping spread her happy messages.

Sally is a graduate of USC with a degree in Fine Art and through the years, has had 26 of her own art galleries.

This certificate may be cut out, framed, and presented to any little girl who promises to honor the princess within her.

Certificate of Merit

_____
(Name)

The girl named above is awarded this Certificate of Merit for honoring the princess within her by promising to be:

*Useful whenever possible

*Grateful at all times

*Friendly to everyone

*Kind and Thoughtful to others

Presented by: _____   Date: _____

Made in the USA
Middletown, DE
16 November 2017